# Picnic at Mudsock Meadow

## Patricia Polacco

PAPERSTAR

The Putnam & Grosset Group

Printed on recycled paper

A PaperStar Book, published in 1997 by The Putnam & Grosset Group,
200 Madison Avenue, New York, NY 10016. PaperStar Books and
the PaperStar logo are trademarks of The Putnam Berkley Group, Inc.
Originally published in 1992 by G. P. Putnam's Sons.
Published simultaneously in Canada.
Printed in the United States of America.

Library of Congress Cataloging-in-Publication Data
Polacco, Patricia. Picnic at Mudsock Meadow/Patricia Polacco. p. cm.
Summary: Having failed to win the pumpkin-carving, pie-eating,
and seed-spitting contests, William hopes to impress
Hester by winning the Dress-Up Competition.
[1. Contests—Fiction. 2. Picnicking—Fiction. 3. Halloween—Fiction.]
I. Title. PZ7.P75186Pi 1992  [E]—dc20  91-7374 CIP AC
ISBN 0-698-11449-3
10 9 8 7 6 5 4 3 2 1

For my mother, Mary Gaw Barber.
*Thanks Mom, for everything.*

It was the day of the annual Halloween picnic at Grange Hall in Mud-sock Meadow. William and his friends stopped a moment just on the edge of the marsh known as Quicksand Bottoms. Most who lived in these parts feared the place. Legend had it that the eerie lights seen coming out of the swamp at night were the ghost of Titus Dinworthy, an old miner who had disappeared there about a hundred years ago.

"Aw, it's just swamp gas," William said with authority.

"Peeeeeee youuuuuuu," Hester Bledden said with a leer, sticking out her tongue. Everyone laughed, and William's face turned as red as a Union City farm-fresh tomato.

When they got to Grange Hall, preparations for the picnic were already in full swing. Mr. Tillwater was cranking the ice-cream freezer for plates-o'-cream to have after the wienie roast. And all over the meadow, folks were gearing up for the contests to come.

"First contest of the day is the pumpkin carving," the mayor's wife boomed.

Here's where I can show that Hester, William thought. But he wasn't very good with his hands.

PUMPKIN CARVING

He always liked science class better than art.

Suddenly he heard Hester yell, "Look at that silly one!" And she was pointing to the pumpkin HE HAD JUST CARVED.

William was still glowering about it at the next contest.

Maybe I'll catch something nice at the fishing booth, he thought. Then I'll go right up to Hester and wave it in her face!

All the other kids were pulling up their lines to find brightly colored little bags of treats tied to the ends. But William's line was tangled, and when he gave it a hard tug, he saw what it was tangled with: Hester Bledden!

Oh no, he thought. Of all people!

"Peeeeee youuuuuu!!" Hester squealed. "Look what I caught... SMELLY OLD WILLIAM!"

My luck's gotta change, William thought as he headed for the pumpkin-seed spitting contest. All the other kids put the seeds in their mouths, took a running start toward the line, and blew the seeds out of their mouths as far as they could. Then Lula Mae Cobb measured the distances and called out the numbers.

As William stepped up to the starting line, he saw Hester looking right at him, and *GULP!* . . . he swallowed the seed.

"You're disqualified, William," Lula Mae guffawed. Now William was really terribly and horribly mortified. And mad as the dickens.

When Margie Biggins called out, "Who's for the tug-o'-war?" William was rarin' to go. Eulaylee Teeter, the mayor's wife, leaned back into the rope around her waist. She had been known in these parts to hold off an opposing team for almost an hour!

So William was pulling pretty hard when he lost his footing and fell backward...and hit the ground right at Hester's feet!

William had one last event...one last chance to save face in front of his friends: the dress-up competition. But when he pulled out the battered sheet that was his ghost costume, all hope vanished. There was Boof Schiffer playing his musical saw, while his brother Bertie ripped newspapers to the beat. And there were the Detweiler sisters with their hair down. They had the longest hair in four states, he figured.

The Wah Ton Yee Girls Auxiliary, Wigwam #2, was dressed as the American flag. William's best friend, Eldon, was dressed as a fat lady. And on the end was Hester. Even William had to admit she looked great as a snake charmer. Jewelry rattled on her neck and ankles, and her vacuum-hose snakes shook their tails.

William knew his dumb old sheet didn't stand a chance.

Suddenly a scream was heard from the end of Grange Hall—just near the window.

"Look! Out there in Quicksand Bottoms!"

The crowd pressed to the window as an eerie light came up out of the swamp.

"It's the ghost of Titus Dinworthy," DeeDee Washburn cried out.

"And he's a-comin' here to get us!" the Detweiler sisters shrieked. The Wah Ton Yee Girls Auxiliary, Wigwam #2, just stood and looked scared. William walked closer to the window.

"All it is is swamp gas," William said in a trembling voice. "I...I'm sure of it."

Everyone went outside to get a better look.

"Be careful, William!" someone called out as he walked toward the light.

"That's close enough, William," another voice said.

Boy, he thought to himself. I sure hope it *is* swamp gas...just like we learned in science. It's called will-o'-the-wisp. "Will-o'-the-wisp," he whispered out loud, to make it seem more convincing.

Then with a loud BLURBLE...BLOOP...BLUBB...BLUBB, the light got bigger and brighter.

"EEEEEEEEEEEE, the ghost!" everyone screamed as they ran toward Grange Hall. William stood his ground. He'd show them. He could just see the headlines in the *Union City Register Bugle Herald Tribune* now: "BOY LOST IN QUICKSAND BOTTOMS—OUTLOOK BLEAK."

But he steeled himself, and with a gulp, he ran toward the light. "Take this, Hester Bledden!" he shouted as he leapt into the air.

KA-BLAP he went, as he landed in the slimy, gooey, glowing gas, mud and swamp water. Then suddenly the light was gone, and so was William.

"OOOOOOOOH...AHHHHHHHHHHH," the crowd intoned, as the wet, slimy, muddy boy climbed out of the bog...unhurt and no worse for wear. But glowing eerily.

This was a Halloween that would go down in the annals of Mudsock Meadow. Not only had William shown uncommon bravery, but he had stopped, once and for all, the talk about Quicksand Bottoms. The will-o'-the-wisp was no longer feared.

As for the dress-up competition, William won it hands down.

"The finest swamp monster I've ever seen!" Mayor Teeter exclaimed.

And Hester? Well, she finally changed her tune.
"My hero," she cooed. And she and William shared a plate-o'-cream.